My Valentine's Gift

The Friends to Lovers Series

by

Reba Bale

Table of Contents

Copyright

About This Book

The only thing worse than getting dumped on Valentine's Day is having it happen in front of the mean girl who terrorized you all through school.

Mia doesn't know what's wrong with her. Every time she thinks she's found "the one" she gets her heart broken. But having her girlfriend announce that she's bad in bed while publicly breaking up with her in a restaurant on Valentine's Day seems like a new low. Especially with her old high school nemesis sitting at the next table.

Colleen has two major regrets in life: not holding onto those Microsoft stocks she inherited from her grandfather, and being a horrible bully to her high school rival Mia. When she runs into Mia in a restaurant right as her girlfriend breaks up with her, she knows this is her second chance to make things right. And maybe even become friends...

Mia might not believe that she's changed, but Colleen's going to do everything she can to convince her former rival that enemies to lovers isn't just something that happens in a romance book.

"My Valentine's Gift" is book eight in the "Friends to Lovers" romantic novella series. Each book in the series is a standalone featuring an LGBTQ couple making the leap from friends to lovers and looking for their "happily ever after". If you like steamy but sweet romances with lots of snark, check out this lesbian romance today.

Author's note: This story contains brief, non-detailed references to eating disorders and past child abuse. Please do not read this book if those are topics that are triggering for you.

Be sure to check out a free preview of Reba Bale's lesbian romance "The Divorcee's First Time" at the end of this book!

Dedication

For everyone who has struggled with an eating disorder. You matter.

Join My Newsletter

Want a free book? Join my newsletter and receive a copy of my book "Hotwife Happy Hour" for free. I promise I will only email you when there are new releases or special sales, usually twice a month.

Visit my newsletter sign-up page[1] at bit.ly/rebabooks to join today.

---

1. https://storyoriginapp.com/giveaways/495308f4-2d9f-11ed-bfd5-c7ccde0cb7e8

Mia

Colleen Murphy was a witness to every major humiliating moment in my life.

When I was eight, she was there pointing and laughing when I got hit in the stomach during dodgeball and puked up my lunchables.

When I was thirteen, Colleen was the one who pointed out that I'd gotten my period for the first time – while I was wearing white shorts. It might have been the first time Aunt Flo visited, but she came with a vengeance, leaving a large red stain that was clearly visible to everyone, especially with Colleen drawing attention to it.

When I was sixteen she was right there when I tripped on my own feet and split my pants on the way down – baring my ass to everyone around. This was shortly after I'd discovered thongs, of course.

When I was eighteen, Colleen happened to be crossing the parking lot when I went into reverse instead of drive and backed into a cop car. I could still hear her cackling as the angry cop jumped out of the car to yell at me.

And when I was thirty-five, she had a ringside seat as my girlfriend of ten months dumped me. In a restaurant. On Valentine's Day. After announcing to everyone that I was bad in bed.

It was safe to say that Colleen and I were lifelong enemies. When we were kids she was the worst kind of bully: the kind who seemed sweet and friendly until she decided you'd wronged her, and then she turned into Cruella de Ville crossed with that chick from Mean Girls. She was always sweet as pie around the adults of course.

She'd seemed to have everything: nice clothes, rich parents, a house on the "good side" of town, perfect skin, and yet it wasn't enough for her. She had to make everyone who wasn't part of her "in" crowd feel like they were inferior.

I hadn't actually seen Colleen Murphy in about seventeen years, not since high school graduation, so I was shocked when I looked over at the table next to mine and saw her sitting there, dining alone. Colleen was never alone. She always either had a posse of her minions surrounding her or some hot jock guy. At least that's how it had been back when we were in school.

We didn't acknowledge each other, but I saw the flash of recognition in her eyes, saw her take stock of me, the same as I did for her.

When we were younger, she was model thin. She wasn't fat now, but she'd definitely filled out a bit. Her breasts and hips were slightly more rounded than they used to be, but her waist was still tiny. She was a petite woman, but she had more muscle tone now, no longer looking like a strong wind might break her in half. Her red hair was cut in a short bob, a big change from the long, silken waves she used to wear. Her face looked almost exactly the same, with super pale skin, green eyes, and a smattering of red freckles across her cute little button nose.

I heard an irritated sigh and turned my attention back to my current girlfriend Gail. Neither of us lived in this neighborhood, but she'd heard about this restaurant from someone at work and had insisted that we come here for Valentine's Day. The food was decent, but a little fancy for my tastes. I was a simple girl. I was perfectly happy with a burger and fries.

"See? This is exactly what I'm talking about," Gail sniped, pinning me with a glare.

"Huh?"

"You never pay attention to me."

"What are you talking about Gail? I always pay attention to you."

I didn't add that it was hard not to when she was always talking. Usually about herself. I couldn't remember the last time she'd asked anything about me. If ever.

"Look Mia, this thing isn't going to work."

"What thing?" I asked in confusion.

Gail gave me an impatient look.

"Us. The truth is I'm not in love with you anymore. I don't know if I ever was."

I set my fork down. I couldn't decide whether I was relieved or irritated. Gail wasn't the woman I was meant to spend the rest of my life with, but I'd thought things were going pretty well between us. Then again, I had a long history of being clueless in relationships.

"Am I living in a bad TV show right now?" I asked, looking around to see if any other diners were watching us. "Where is this coming from?"

"Don't make this harder than it already is, Mia. I'm dumping you. Deal with it."

Gail stood up.

"Is there someone else?" I asked.

It was the only thing that made sense. Gail was, as they say, a stage four clinger. I'd always assumed that when it was time to break up, I'd have to be the one to do it. Her breaking up with me first was the last thing I'd expected to happen.

"I'm going to spend some time with myself," Gail said.

She didn't meet my eyes, telling me that she was lying. She'd found someone else. I wondered if it was someone I knew. We'd originally met because we had a lot of mutual friends.

"Who is she?"

"No one you know. I've finally figured out what I want in a relationship," Gail continued, her voice rising. "I want to be with someone who fulfils all my needs, especially in the bedroom. That's definitely not you. You're terrible in bed."

Several heads turned in our direction at that announcement, including Colleen's. Wasn't this just the perfect ending to a lackluster relationship?

"Goodbye Mia, have a nice life."

My now ex-girlfriend flounced out of the restaurant, leaving me with a red face and an unpaid dinner check. Nice of her to order an expensive meal and eat it before breaking up with me and doing a dine and dash.

What the fuck had just happened?

I drained the rest of my wine, even though I didn't really like the taste of it. Gail was the one who liked wine, and I'd just gone along with it. What was wrong with me? How had I become this woman who was so desperate for love that I deferred to whatever woman I was dating at the time? I used to be strong. Opinionated. A free spirit. And now I was just...pathetic.

I sighed and lowered my chin to my chest, staring at the tablecloth. I felt someone stop by my table and looked up to see Colleen Murphy standing there. I expected to see the smug mocking face that had tormented me all through school but instead she looked sympathetic. Kind even.

"You can do way better than that bitch," she murmured. "How about we get out of here and get a drink?"

Colleen

When I came to this restaurant tonight, I'd had no idea it was Valentine's Day.

I had just gotten back from a grueling business trip and after finding a mostly empty refrigerator, I was looking for a good meal. This restaurant was only a few blocks from my house, and I came here often.

When I walked in and saw the place filled with couples, red heart centerpieces on every table, I'd almost left again. But I was hungry, and after working hard to learn how to listen to my body's signals and nourish myself with food, I wasn't going to deprive myself of a good meal just because I was going to have to eat alone on Valentine's Day. I didn't care about the stupid holiday anyway.

I hadn't really noticed the other diners, lost in my own thoughts as I ate my dinner, until a woman raised her voice at a nearby table. I'd looked up and been shocked to see Mia Hernandez, former classmate, and the person that I'd bullied for years.

I wasn't proud of it. I didn't even realize it was bullying at the time, too caught up in my own family drama. I'd just seen someone who didn't give a shit what people thought about her, someone who was well-fed, happy looking, and had a nice circle of friends who actually liked her for who she was, and I'd hated her immediately.

Mia's name had come up in therapy a couple of times last year. I hadn't thought about her in years, wrapped up in my own life. But something had come up that reminded me of her, and suddenly I had the realization that I'd been an asshole to her. I'd been determined to apologize if I ever saw her again. I was even contemplating going to our twentieth high school reunion in a couple of years for the express purpose of apologizing to Mia. But now, here she was.

I'd never done a ten-step program, but this was still my chance to make amends.

She looked almost the same as the last time I'd seen her, at high school graduation. She still had those thick dark brown locks that hung past her shoulders. Her light brown skin was clear, with almond shaped brown eyes, a pert little nose, and a mouth that was just a little too wide for her face. Her body was curvy and lush and womanly.

I realized with a jolt that I was attracted to her. I hadn't realized I was a lesbian until I was a sophomore in college – or maybe it was more accurate to say that I'd realized it but not accepted it until then – but now I wondered if on some level I'd been attracted to her back when we were teenagers. Being attracted to Mia felt very familiar to me. Maybe my immature teenaged brain had subconsciously pushed her away precisely because I liked her so much.

I winced as the woman she was dining with announced to the restaurant that she was breaking up with Mia because she was bad in bed. I recognized the type of person Mia's girlfriend was: narcissistic, self-absorbed, needing to insult others to make herself feel better. I'd been raised by that type of person, and in many ways, I used to be that type of person too.

The woman flounced away in a huff, leaving Mia sitting alone. She drank down her glass of red wine, grimacing a bit as if she didn't like the taste of it. Screwing up my courage, I walked over to her table.

"You can do way better than that bitch," I told her softly, not wanting to contribute to her embarrassment. "How about we get out of here and get a drink?"

"I think I've had enough abuse for one night, thanks."

Mia's tone was bitter, not that I blamed her. I plopped myself down in the chair her girlfriend had vacated and met her angry gaze, doing my best to radiate kindness.

"I know I was a total bitch to you throughout school," I told her earnestly. "But I'm not that person anymore. I didn't come over here to harass you."

"Why did you come over?" she asked.

"You looked like you could use a friend." When Mia didn't respond I added, "I know a great hole-in-the-wall bar close to here that makes good, strong drinks. Come have a drink. It's on me."

I thought she'd refuse, but after a long moment she nodded. "Okay. But I'm going to need several drinks after the day I've had."

"You got it, Mia."

We each paid our checks and headed outside. It was February in Seattle, so it was cold and rainy, the kind of cold, damp weather that got into your bones. We zipped up our almost identical black Columbia Sportswear raincoats, put up the hoods, and walked the few blocks to Miller's.

I pushed on the heavy wooden door, holding it open for Mia. She looked around in surprise, taking in the scarred bar with a flickering "Miller Light" sign behind it, the battered jukebox in the corner, and the mismatched tables and chairs.

"This isn't the kind of place I'd expect you to go to," Mia said.

No doubt she'd expected me to bring her to the kind of place that had fancy appetizers and appletinis and men in suits looking to score.

Miller's was the quintessential dive bar, and I loved it. Big Bob Miller ambled out from behind the bar and gave me a bear hug, lifting me off my feet. Big Bob used to be a football player in his youth. He was tall, broad, covered in tattoos, and as intimidating as hell if you didn't know him. He kept a baseball bat behind the bar for unruly patrons, and he wasn't afraid to use it. Despite his appearance, he was a great guy. A gentle giant. And in many ways, he'd been a surrogate father to me.

"Colleen sweetheart, it's good to see you. It's been a while."

By "a while" he meant two weeks.

At Mia's raised eyebrows, I explained, "I worked here for several years."

"And she's one of my best customers now," Big Bob said, sticking out a beefy hand. "I'm Big Bob."

"I'm Mia, nice to meet you Big Bob."

"Whaddaya girls want tonight?" Big Bob asked me, crunching his words together as he often did.

"We'll take a pitcher of Long Island Iced Tea," I said. I glanced over at Mia. "Is that okay, or would you rather have something else?"

"Nope, that's great."

"Should we grab a booth?" I suggested.

Mia and I headed to a booth in the corner. We sat silently until Big Bob returned with our pitcher of Long Island Iced Tea. I poured us each a glass of the strong cocktail, sliding one towards Mia.

"I already got a basket of fries going for you Colleen," Big Bob told me with a smile.

"You know me so well," I returned his smile.

"You want anything else right now?"

I glanced over at Mia, who shook her head.

"No thanks. That'll be good for now," I told Big Bob.

Mia leaned forward, studying me carefully. "You seem different. The Colleen Murphy I used to know wouldn't eat fries or be caught dead in a place like this."

"Well, a lot of things have changed over the last seventeen years," I replied. "Most of all me. And I'd like to apologize for being such an insensitive bitch when we were younger. I was awful to you, and you did nothing to deserve that. I want you to know that I'm sincerely sorry for my actions."

Mia

I swear my jaw damn near dropped to the table at Colleen's words. Sure, I knew a lot of years had passed since we'd last seen each other, but I would never have expected Colleen to be so different. It wasn't just her appearance or her behavior, her energy was different now. Calmer. More mature. Less toxic.

"Why?" I asked.

"Why am I apologizing, or why was I such a bully?"

I took a sip of my Long Island Iced Tea. It was delicious. And strong as hell. I needed to be careful, or this thing would knock me on my ass.

"I guess both."

"I'd always hoped I'd run into you some day," Colleen told me. "I owe you an apology. I was...well, things weren't good at home when I was a kid. It messed with my head, and my priorities. I truly am sorry, Mia. I feel terrible about being such a bully."

We paused as Big Bob brought us over a giant basket of crispy French fries, two small plates, and bottles of ketchup and mustard. Colleen smiled happily, squeezing some ketchup onto a plate, adding mustard, then using a fry to swirl it all together. She popped the fry into her mouth, eyes closing happily, and I felt a weird little tingle in my core. She was really cute.

"All the years I knew you, I don't think I ever saw you eat anything but carrot sticks and celery, and maybe some grilled chicken. Even in grade school you were eating like a rabbit," I reminisced.

"That's because my mom was an Almond Mom."

"What does that mean?" I asked.

"Have you seen this on TikTok?" When I shook my head she continued, "An Almond Mom is a woman who pushes disordered eating on her kid, usually a daughter. She's so obsessed with staying thin and keeping her daughter thin that she restricts food. I was on a strict diet my entire childhood."

"Oh my God, your mother didn't let you eat?" I asked, completely appalled. "Is that why you were so skinny?"

Colleen nodded. "I believed what she told me, that I needed to be constantly vigilant or I'd become hugely fat. I'd eat a couple of almonds and think I needed to run on the treadmill for an hour. I never put anything but vinegar on my salads, and I avoided carbs like they were the plague. I was undernourished, and eventually my brain got so fucked up I went full on anorexic. It got worse as I got older. By the time I went away to college I had dieted myself down to ninety-five pounds, terrified that I was going to gain the freshman fifteen."

"Wow." Honestly, I didn't know what else to say.

"When I was in my sophomore year of college it finally came to a head. I passed out in the hallway, and they took me to the ER. The hospital staff saw my emaciated figure and realized right away what was going on with me. My doctor pulled some strings to get me into a place that could help me, and I agreed to do in-patient treatment for my eating disorder."

She took another drink of her Long Island Iced Tea. "I spent a full year doing in-patient treatment. It saved my life."

"And now?"

"Now I eat to nourish my body." She dipped a fry in her ketchup/mustard mix with a smile. "And sometimes I eat things that have no nutritional value, solely because it appeals to me. Like these delicious French fries. But enough about me, tell me about that horrible girl you were dating."

I grabbed a handful of fries and dropped them on my plate to soak up the alcohol that was already going to my head.

"Honestly, I never liked her that much."

"Then why were you dating her?"

"She was a placeholder." At Colleen's questioning look I explained, "A person you date while you're waiting for the right person to come along. I somehow keep ending up with women like that. I think I'm in love with them or something, then later I realize that I was really just settling, biding my time with them in case someone better doesn't come along."

"Well, stop it." Her voice was firm, but then her lips quirked like she'd said something funny.

"What?"

"Did you ever see that old comedy sketch with Bob Newhart? He's a therapist and a woman comes to him for help with phobias, and whatever she says she's afraid of, he just yells 'stop it' like, it's that simple. So...stop it!"

Then she started giggling and I caught my breath. Colleen smiling was a sight to behold. I'd never seen this genuine smile on her before. It made me smile back.

"I never knew that you were so weird," I teased.

"Oh, you have no idea."

We spent the next two hours sucking down Long Island Iced Teas and making our way through the gigantic basket of fries. While we drank we caught each other up on our lives.

I learned that Colleen had been estranged from her parents since shortly before she finished her eating disorder treatment.

"My mother couldn't stand the fact that I'd gained weight in the program, and my father wasn't interested in having a daughter who's a lesbian," she explained. "I came out to them when I was in treatment. As far as my father was concerned, being gay was a sin. Being a drunken, abusive asshole was okay though. My parents told me not to bother coming home, so I cashed out some Microsoft stock my grandfather gave me when I turned eighteen, dropped out of college, and moved out on my own after I finished treatment."

I knew there was more to the story, but she changed the subject and I let it slide. She would tell me more when she was ready. I paused, realizing that, to my shock, I really wanted to spend more time with her.

"Wow, you really should have held onto that Microsoft stock," I joked, trying to lighten the mood. "You'd probably be loaded now."

"No kidding."

Our conversation turned to our careers.

Colleen shared that she'd never gone back to college. She did a full year of in-patient treatment, then moved to an apartment near Miller's where she still lived now. She waitressed here at the bar for several years then took a paralegal course and eventually got a better paying job at a law firm downtown.

"I could afford a nicer place now," she told me. "But I really love this neighborhood and my apartment suits me fine. Eventually I'm hoping to buy a house nearby. What about you, Mia? What have you been doing since high school?"

"I went to U-Dub," I told her, the local name for University of Washington. "I majored in social work."

"Oh wow, that's so great. What made you pick social work?"

"My mom was a social worker, and she always told me how there were so many black and brown kids in the system, but so few staff who came from their community who were in a position to help them. She inspired me to follow in her footsteps."

"I love that," Colleen said. I noticed that her voice was slurring a bit now. "Where do you work?"

"I'm in the social services department at the children's hospital."

"Are you and your mom still close?"

I smiled. "Yeah, my mom's my best friend."

My head buzzed, and I realized that I was way more intoxicated than I thought I was. Those Long Island Iced Teas packed a punch.

"I supposed I should be heading home," I said. "I'll have to call an Uber or something. There's no way I should be driving tonight."

"Why don't you come home with me?"

Colleen

I tried not to be hurt when Mia made an appalled face at my invitation.

"I'm sorry, but I just got out of a relationship a few hours ago. As you know."

That wasn't why I'd invited her to come back to my place. Not that I would mind sleeping with Mia. She was hot as hell, and all night I'd felt a hum of attraction between us. But apparently it was one-sided. Even if it wasn't, we were both too drunk for anything to happen.

"I meant you could stay in my guest room, so you don't have to drive," I clarified, keeping my voice neutral.

She rolled her eyes at herself. "Sorry, my thought processes are not at their fastest right now. I haven't been this wasted in years."

"Let's get you to bed then," I said. "Do you need to go to work in the morning?"

We both stood up, and I felt my head spin. I saw Mia grip the table, like maybe she was having the same issue.

"I'm going to call out sick when we get back to your place. I have a suspicion that I'm going to be hungover tomorrow."

"Come on then."

We walked the few blocks to my apartment, both of us lost in thought. This late, the streets were mostly empty, and we got to my building quickly.

"Nice place," Mia said, looking around my second floor walk-up apartment.

I felt a flush of pleasure. It wasn't much, but it was mine. My parents would be appalled at this place. It would be too small and middle class for their tastes. It didn't have marble floors or stainless steel appliances or the latest electronics. But I knew better than anyone that a fancy house didn't mean a happy home.

"The guest room is here," I said, leading Mia to the appropriate doorway. "The bathroom is right next door, and I'm across the hall. I'll get you a towel and bring you some sweats to sleep in."

She was wearing a dress and chunky heels for her Valentine's date. Her outfit was super hot but wouldn't be comfortable to sleep in.

"Thanks." She grabbed my hand, meeting my eyes. "I really appreciate you cheering me up, Colleen. I'm glad we ran into each other."

"Me too," I said, ignoring the little zing I felt from her hand. "Good night."

I woke up early out of years of habit, glad I'd downed some ibuprofen and a bottle of water before I went to bed. I'd brought some for Mia too, but when I came into the guest room she was already out cold, so I'd just left them on the bedside table for when she woke up.

I glanced in the open door. She was still asleep, laying on her back with her arms and legs spread wide like a starfish. It was adorable. She was adorable. But her reaction last night had been clear: she wasn't interested in me and even if she was, she'd just got dumped the night before. She needed some time to get over her heartbreak. Or at least being humiliated in the restaurant.

Stop watching her sleep like some kind of a creeper, I chastised myself.

Pulling away from Mia's doorway, I made a full pot of coffee instead of the half pot I usually made, leaving half the pot for Mia. If she wasn't a coffee drinker, I could heat up the rest for tomorrow. After taking a quick shower, I got ready for work, grabbing a travel cup full of black coffee and packing a Greek yogurt and an apple to bring for breakfast.

Since Mia was still asleep, I wrote her a note and taped it to the bathroom mirror where she was bound to find it.

Mia, It was fun reconnecting last night. I had to go to work. I left you coffee in the pot and there's fruit and yogurt in the fridge if you're hungry. There's a fresh toothbrush in the drawer next to the bathroom sink. Please make yourself at home, just lock the door when you leave. Give me a call sometime, I'd love to hang out again. Colleen

I spent the rest of the day thinking about Mia, wondering when she got up, how she was feeling, and whether she would call me. I'd realized last night that I'd had a huge crush on Mia since at least junior high, and in my self-loathing about being a lesbian, I'd been super rude to her as if to prove to myself she wasn't someone I should be with.

That was something I'd definitely have to unpack more with my therapist this week. Even though I had completed treatment fifteen years ago, I still went to therapy a couple of times a month to keep my mental health in good shape.

After work I hurried home, half hoping that Mia was still there, but of course she wasn't. Why would she just hang out at my apartment all day? That would be weird.

Later that night I received a text.

Unknown Number: *Hey Colleen it's Mia. Thank you so much for everything last night. Seriously, you took a shit night and turned it into something fun. I really appreciate that.*

Colleen: *I'm glad, I had fun too. How are you feeling?*

Mia: *Better now but I was a little shaky this morning. I'm too old to drink that much, LOL.*

Colleen: *Big Bob's Long Island Iced Teas pack a punch, but I love them.*

Mia: *It didn't help that I had half a bottle of wine at dinner before I started drinking with you.*

Colleen: *LOL*

Mia: *Remember last night we were talking about 80s movies? I noticed that Sixteen Candles is playing at that theater downtown with the couches and dinner service. I thought we could go this weekend if you were free?*

Colleen: *I'd love to. What day works?*

Mia: *I usually go to church and have brunch with my mom on Sunday mornings, so how about Saturday? There's a five o'clock show.*

Colleen: *Sounds great. How about I meet you there at 4:45?*

Mia: *That works. I'll reserve tickets and see you then. I'm looking forward to hanging out with you again.*

As I closed my phone screen, I had to smile. I was in the friend zone, but at least I'd get to spend time with Mia. For right now, that would be enough.

Mia

"What did you do last night, *mija*?"

I looked across the table at my mom, almost a mirror image of me. She'd gotten pregnant when she was only eighteen and had me at nineteen. We'd practically grown up together, and given how well she was aging, people often mistook us for sisters.

My dad had never been in the picture, signing away his parental rights when he learned my mom was pregnant, so it had always just been the two of us in our little family. Although we were also lucky to have my abuela and about a million cousins who lived in the city.

"I hung out with Colleen," I said, answering my mother's question.

"You girls have been spending a lot of time together," Mom observed, sliding over a bowl of pozole.

I inhaled, breathing in the scent of meat and spices from the stew. "Yeah, we have now that you mention it."

"Any sparkage there?"

"Not really."

Mom pinned me with a disbelieving look. She knew me too well.

"I don't think she sees me that way," I added.

"But *you* see *her* that way?"

"Yeah, but I'm afraid I'm doing that thing I always do, where I monkey bar from one woman to the next."

For the last ten years, I'd been a serial monogamist, moving from one serious relationship right into the next without so much as a break in between. After my break-up from Gail, I'd resolved to spend some time working on myself, figuring out why it felt so important for me to always be in a relationship. To figure out why I felt compelled to change myself to reflect who I was with.

While I was doing some introspection, it was a good time to develop a new friendship.

Being friends with Colleen was simple. We'd fallen into it way easier than I ever would have guessed. She was so different from the girl I'd gone to school with all those years. School Colleen had been a judgmental bully, worried only about appearances and having the fanciest things money could buy. Current Day Colleen shopped at thrift stores and ate burgers and accepted people just like they were. It was a remarkable transformation.

"You broke up with that selfish girl, what? Like three months ago now?"

Mom had never liked Gail, which should have been a red flag. Mom had a good instinct for people.

"Yeah."

"Seems like that's enough time to get over someone," Mom said decisively. "You should bring Colleen over to dinner next Sunday."

"As a friend?"

"If you say so, *mija*."

Colleen was thrilled when I told her that my Mom wanted to meet her. I knew she still beat herself up about how she'd acted towards me in school, but knowing her as well as I did now, her behavior back then made sense. The poor girl was constantly hungry and being physically and mentally abused by her parents. I was a social worker, I'd seen the way that victims of childhood abuse often acted out by exerting control over others or treating them the same way they'd been treated at home.

I'd forgiven Colleen, even if she hadn't forgiven herself.

I picked Colleen up and we met my Mom at her neighborhood parish, St. Guadalupe's. As a lesbian, I had a conflicted relationship with Catholicism. It was hard to justify the Church's positions on LGBTQ rights and reproductive justice. On the other hand, I'd been going to this church since I was a little girl, and I found the ritual comforting and familiar. Plus, the pastor, Father John, had been there forever and fully accepted me despite my sexual orientation.

"I was raised Catholic too," Colleen said when I'd offered to pick her up after church instead of dragging her with us. "I don't mind coming with you. It'll be nice."

We met my mom outside the building in a covered courtyard near the parking lot. She pulled Colleen into a big hug, because that's just who my Mom was. She'd hug anyone. My friend looked shocked, then happy as she relaxed into the hug. Mom was a great hugger.

"It's nice to meet you after hearing about you all these years," Mom told her.

Colleen's fair complexion reddened with embarrassment. "I wasn't very nice to your daughter when we were kids."

Mom patted her shoulder. "It's more important how you act as an adult."

The three of us went inside for Mass, then walked the four blocks to Mom's house. Years ago, she'd bought a tiny bungalow in this neighborhood, which was all she could afford at the time. Like a lot of places in Seattle, Mom's neighborhood had seen a lot of redevelopment – or gentrification, depending on your point of view – and now what had been a primarily Mexican neighborhood was becoming a bit more white hipster. But Mom was still happy living here.

We all helped my mother to put the finishing touches on brunch, then sat down to eat our meal. As usual, everything was delicious. Mom had been taught to cook by my abuela, and she was quite good at it, unlike me.

While we ate, Mom did that thing she did where she grilled someone without them having any idea they were being grilled. Mom was incredibly skilled at getting information out of people, without her questions seeming nearly as intrusive as they were. By the time she was done with Colleen, Mom had ferreted out her entire life story, and the two of them were chatting like lifelong best friends.

When brunch was over, Colleen and I worked together to do the dishes. We stood side by side, with me washing and Colleen drying, our fingers occasionally touching as we passed a dish between us. Something about having Colleen here was messing with my mind. It was easy to forget we were just friends as we did something so domestic.

"Hey Mia?"

I turned at the sound of Colleen's soft voice and our eyes met and held, something undefinable running between us.

"Thanks for bringing me here," she said quietly. "I appreciate feeling like a part of your family, even for a few hours."

I couldn't help it, I pulled her into my arms, hugging her close. Her arms wrapped around my waist, holding onto me like she'd never let go, a world of unspoken emotion flowing between us in that simple connection. Having Colleen in my arms felt incredibly right.

When we pulled apart, she looked like she was trying not to cry. I cupped her cheek with my hand.

"You're welcome to hang out with my family any time. Next time I'll bring you to meet my abuela, that'll scare you off from families for a while."

Colleen laughed, breaking the seriousness of the moment. As she stepped away, I realized I was in more trouble than I'd thought. I didn't just have a crush on my friend, I was in love with her.

Colleen

Spending time with Mia's mom had been a revelation. I'd always isolated myself to some extent. As a kid because of the shame of my family, and as an adult because of my fear that I was too broken and somehow unlovable. Feeling the easy love between mother and daughter showed me how things could be.

Hugging Mia in the kitchen had showed me something else: I'd somehow fallen in love with her.

Sometimes I got the impression that she felt the same way about me, but I couldn't tell for sure. I'd never been good at reading people, not really. I'd always tended to live in my head, focused inwardly.

But I'd noticed over the last few weeks that there was an increase in the number of "moments" between us: a look that lasted a little too long, a touch on the shoulder or the arm, one of us sitting just a smidge too close. Maybe I was reading too much into it though.

Mia had been hurt. By me. By previous girlfriends. I wasn't sure she'd make the first move even if she was interested. And I wasn't sure if she wanted me to cross the line and make a move. If I was misreading things, I'd lose someone who'd become a good friend over the last few months. It was so confusing.

One Friday night we met up at Miller's, sitting in what I thought of as "our" booth, back in the corner. We'd mostly forgone the Long Island Iced Teas since our first visit. Tonight I was drinking a vodka cranberry and Mia was drinking a margarita as we shared a basket of fries. I repressed a smile as Mia mixed ketchup and mustard on her plate to make a fry sauce. She'd thought it was weird when she first saw me do it, until she tried it, then she was a convert.

I raised my vodka cranberry. "Let's toast."

"What are we toasting to?" Mia asked.

"Life. Happiness. Friendship."

"Cheers."

We both took a healthy sip of our drinks, gazes fixed on one another.

"Mia? Hey!"

I looked up to see two women approaching our table, holding hands.

"Miranda, Elizabeth, this is a surprise. What are you guys doing in this neighborhood?" Mia greeted them.

"Elizabeth had an artist event nearby," Miranda explained, nodding towards her companion.

Mia sent me a look, then asked, "Would you like to join us?"

"Sure."

Mia slid out of the booth, letting the couple take her side while she slid in next to me.

"This is my friend Colleen," Mia said. "Colleen, this is Miranda, we work together in the hospital's social work department. And her girlfriend, Elizabeth."

"Nice to meet you both," I said politely.

The other couple looked between us curiously. "Are you two together?" Elizabeth asked.

For some reason we both paused, our eyes meeting for a long moment, before we said, almost in unison, "Just friends."

Elizabeth looked suspicious but didn't say anything else. I wondered if the other couple could pick up on the vibes between us, or if I was just imagining it. It felt like the more time we spent together, the more the attraction grew between Mia and me, at least on my side.

Big Bob came by and got everyone's drink orders, then we all chatted for a while. At some point Mia moved closer to me, her leg pressing against mine, setting off a continuous buzzing feeling along my skin even through the two layers of clothing between us.

I glanced down and realized that Mia's nipples were at full attention, and there was the slightest bit of tension around her jaw, as if touching me was affecting her as much as it was affecting me. Deciding to take a risk, I moved my hand beneath the table and settled it on her thigh.

I heard Mia's soft intake of breath, saw the fluttering of her pulse in her neck.

"How did you two get together?" I asked, distracting myself for a moment so I wouldn't lean over and kiss Mia.

"Elizabeth and I were college roommates," Miranda said. "Best friends, actually. We had feelings for each other but neither of us wanted to risk our friendship by exploring those feelings. We finally let ourselves go, and we had one night together, then Elizabeth immediately ditched me and married a guy."

I raised my eyebrows in surprise.

"I was young and stupid," Elizabeth explained. "My parents were rich and all about appearances, and I didn't want to disappoint them or cause drama. I knew they'd freak out if they thought I was a lesbian."

"You *were* a lesbian," Miranda reminded her.

"Yeah, but I wasn't strong enough to come out to them yet."

"What happened?" I asked, struck by our similar background stories.

"I finally came out to them and ditched my husband. My parents disowned me, so I moved up north and became an artist and tarot card reader. Then a couple of years ago I was at a lesbian spirituality retreat at Sagebrush down in Oregon. Miranda was there too and we...reconnected."

"And lived happily ever after," Miranda teased, laying her head on Elizabeth's shoulder.

They were adorable together, and so clearly in love. I glanced over at Mia, wondering if she was seeing the parallels in their story and ours, the way I was. She was wearing a simple cotton skirt that fell just above her knees when she was standing and bared her some of her thigh sitting.

Mia hadn't shoved my hand off her thigh, making me think it was okay to take things to the next level. I hoped I wasn't wrong. I pretended to pay attention to a story Elizabeth was telling us about a weird tarot card session she'd done recently while slowly, so slowly, sliding the cotton skirt a little higher on Mia's thigh. Her strong leg muscles twitched beneath my fingers.

When she didn't bat my hand away, I shifted it a little higher, a little farther in, so I could touch the silky skin of her inner thigh. She choked on her drink a little, but after a long, pregnant pause, she opened her legs slightly, giving me access.

I'd never been one to waste an opportunity.

Acting casual, I slid my hand up a bit more, until my pinky finger rested against the crotch of her panties. Mia was breathing a bit heavier now, even while she struggled to keep up with the conversation.

Fortunately, Elizabeth and Miranda were chatty and didn't seem to require a lot of back and forth.

I rubbed my pinky finger up and down the fabric, then rotated my wrist so I could cup her mound. Her panties were soaking wet, and I felt a surge of power and excitement. Mia wasn't unaffected. Her panties were as wet as I know mine were. I squeezed her ever so slightly, and her thighs snapped together, trapping my hand between her legs.

"You know, I'm kind of tired," Mia said, interrupting Elizabeth mid-sentence. "It was nice running into you two, but I'd better get going."

"I'll go with you," I said quickly.

We said our goodbyes to Miranda and Elizabeth, promising to get together again some time, paid our tab, and left the bar. As soon as we cleared the door, Mia grabbed my hand and pulled me around the corner of the building. Before I could take my next breath, she'd pushed me against the brick wall, her hands on my shoulders. Her mouth lowered, and then my friend was kissing me.

Her lips were soft and firm as they pressed against mine. I slid my hands around her waist, pulling her closer, and she sucked my bottom lip into her mouth. I sighed, and her tongue swooped into my mouth, sliding against mine.

She kissed me until we were both gasping for breath, then pulled away, resting her forehead against mine, our eyes meeting in the dim light.

"What was that?" she asked finally.

"I don't know, but you started it," I teased, lightening the mood.

"YOU started it with your roving hands," she reminded me.

I looked up at her through my eyelashes, my smile turning naughty.

"Well, I'd like to finish it."

Mia

I wasn't sure how it happened, but somehow I was making out with Colleen in the alley. It was hot as hell, but a little confusing.

When I'd felt her hand on my thigh, I'd thought she was just being friendly. When her fingers slid underneath my skirt and between my legs, it became clear her intentions were more than friendly. Just sitting pressed up against her had made my body vibrate with awareness, but feeling her fingers against the crotch of my panties had damn near made me come on the spot.

I'd wanted her for what felt like forever. I'd promised myself that I wouldn't cross the invisible boundary that would change or relationship, but now that Colleen had made the first move, I was free to act on my feelings.

I pulled her into the alley without a conscious thought, just a biological imperative to get my lips on hers. And now that we'd kissed for the first time, I knew one thing for sure: Colleen was mine. I'd never had a kiss like that. Never felt so instantly alive as I had when our lips touched.

When Colleen gave me a look that was pure sin and whispered, "I'd like to finish it," I was done. I immediately forgot all the reasons that I'd been resisting this.

"Are you sure?" I asked. "Be sure. Because I love having you as a friend, and if things don't work out, I don't want to lose you."

"I'm sure."

By unspoken agreement, we headed in the direction of Colleen's apartment, our fingers threaded together, hands swinging between us. It was a dry spring night, but there was a nip in the air. I took a deep breath, filling my lungs and feeling hopeful for the first time in a long time.

As soon as the door to Colleen's apartment closed, we were on each other like two horny teenagers. Our bodies met in a clash of teeth and hands, Colleen's breasts pressed against my ribcage, mine against her collarbones, our pelvises grinding against each other.

"You're wearing too many clothes," Colleen gasped as we pulled apart.

Before I could comprehend her words or her intentions, she'd whipped my shirt over my head and unclasped my bra.

"Wow, that was impressive," I teased as my heavy breasts fell from their confinement.

Colleen moved forward, gripping my hips as her mouth closed around one nipple, circling it with her tongue. I slid my fingers into her fine, straight hair, so different from my own, and pulled her closer. She responded by sucking my nipple and areola deep into her mouth, drawing on me in a way that made my already-damp panties completely soaked as my core flooded with moisture.

I whined as she released my breast, then relaxed as she returned to give the other one the same attention. My breasts had always been sensitive, and under Colleen's talented mouth, they felt like they were literally on fire.

"Colleen," I gasped. "Let's go into the bedroom."

"I thought you'd never ask," she teased, dragging me behind her to the main bedroom.

I'd stayed over at her place several times over the past few months, always in the guest room, but this was the first time I'd been in her bedroom. She'd made a little sanctuary in here, painting it in soft earthen colors, adding comfortable furniture, pillows, and bedding, all decorated with a light floral motif. She swept the pile of throw pillows off her bed, sending them cascading to the floor.

"Take off your skirt and panties. I want to taste your pussy."

My eyes widened. I hadn't seen this bossy side of Colleen since we were kids, and unlike when I was younger, I kind of liked it. At least in this context.

I slid my skirt and panties down, leaving me completely naked. The look she sent me was smoldering.

"You're beautiful, even more beautiful than I imagined." She pressed on my sternum, encouraging me to get on the bed. "And believe me when I say I imagined it a lot."

I sat on the bed, scooting back and lowering myself to my elbows. Still fully dressed, Colleen crawled up the bed, moving between my legs, shoving them open even more with her narrow shoulders. She glanced up at me from my center, then lowered her head, sucking first one pussy lip, then the other, into her mouth. No one had ever done that before, but it felt incredible.

Her hands moved to my legs, moving them even wider, then she gripped my lower lips, one in each hand, opened me up more, and gave me a long swipe of her tongue right up the center of my channel. My hips lifted of their own accord, and Colleen's grip on my thighs tightened.

"Be still," she said, her voice firm.

I shivered.

She began licking me up and down in earnest, her talented tongue moving from just above my ass, up to my clit and down again, tasting me, teasing me, driving me crazy.

"Colleen," I whined. My hands went to her head, trying to direct her to where I needed her most.

She complied, turning her focus to my clit. It was already swollen and sensitive from what felt like hours of foreplay. Months of foreplay. She circled my clit with her tongue, adding pressure, then tapped it a few times with the tip, repeating the sequence over and over again until I was babbling incoherently.

I felt her slide a finger into my dripping channel, then she added a second one. She started stroking in and out while continuing to lick and suck on my clit. Colleen bent her fingers, searching out my G-spot, and when she found it, she pressed her fingers against the rough patch while biting down lightly on my clit.

"Colleen!"

That was all I got out before I was flying, my soul seeming to leave my body as wave after wave of pleasure rolled through me. I shook beneath her, but Colleen held me firm, sucking and licking and stroking me until the tremors stopped and I collapsed, completely spent.

"Jesus," I whispered. "You're so good at that."

Colleen kissed her way up my stomach, across my breasts, over my clavicles, to my lips. I returned the kiss, my fingers moving into her soft hair. When we broke apart, she slid to my side, head resting on my shoulder. I looked down, realizing she was still fully dressed.

"Why are you still wearing clothes?" I asked in confusion.

"I was in too much of a hurry to eat you out," she said lightly. "I've been dying to do that. For years."

"We've only been friends for a few months," I protested.

She lifted up on her elbow, looking down at me. "When I was in high school, I sometimes fantasized about you. Sometimes I had dreams where I was kissing you," she confided. "I was so confused by it. I'd been told being a lesbian was wrong, yet none of the guys I dated made me as excited as Fantasy Mia."

"Sounds like Fantasy Mia was a total stud, or whatever the female equivalent to that is."

"You have no idea."

Colleen

Saying that having sex with Mia was life changing was not an exaggeration. Even just eating her out, bringing her pleasure, was enough to fundamentally change everything I'd ever believed about intimacy. I'd heard people say that there was a difference between having sex and making love, and now I finally understood what they meant. Because we'd just made love. And I hoped we'd do it again.

Mia lay on her back, her light brown skin a contrast against the stark white of the sheets. Her dark hair was spread out on the pillow in a riot of curls. I'd always been jealous of her thick, curly hair, so different from my own red hair, which was thin and fine. It was thicker and fuller now that I gave my body nutrients, but I was never going to be in a shampoo commercial, that's for sure.

"Now that I've caught my breath," Mia spoke up, interrupting my reverie. "How about you take off your clothes and get on up here?"

She pointed at her face, one eyebrow raised suggestively.

"You want me to ride your face?" I clarified, my face heating.

I'd never done that with anyone before, man or woman. I'd always worried that I was too heavy, or that it was an unattractive angle, but with Mia, the idea sounded as appealing as hell. I trusted her enough to try it.

I slid off the bed, removing my clothes. I saw Mia looking at my body, studying my slim arms, strong legs, the gentle curves of my narrow hips and small breasts. Years ago, I would have been appalled to be this size, thinking I was fat. My mother would have confirmed that, encouraging me to do a "water cleanse", one of the many ways she restricted food for both of us. Now I was well enough to recognize that while I was smaller than the average woman, I also was strong and curvy, like a woman should be.

"Come on baby," Mia encouraged. "I want a taste."

I climbed on the bed and moved until my knees were on either side of her head. Gripping the wrought iron headboard behind her, I slowly lowered my pelvis until my pussy just touched her face.

Mia gripped my hips, bringing me farther down, exploring my folds with her tongue.

"Delicious," she whispered.

I wondered what I tasted like. I'd been with enough women to know that we all had our own unique taste.

Mia's tongue turned rough, pushing in between my lower lips, pressing firmly against my clit. My heart was pounding so loud I could hear my pulse in my ears.

"Oh God."

Suddenly her tongue speared my channel, moving in and out of me like my fingers had done with hers. Unable to hold back anymore, I ground my pussy into her face, totally lost in the haze of pleasure.

One hand left my hip, sliding to my center, and Mia caught my clit between two fingers while she continued to fuck me with her tongue. Her fingers pressed together, pinching my clit, and I came with a long wail.

"Mia! Oh my God!"

I made a sound that I'd never made before, somewhere between a wail and a screech. My hands were gripping the headboard so tightly my fingers were turning white. All the blood in my body seemed to pool in my pelvis as I bucked against Mia's face and rode out my orgasm.

I finally collapsed, and realizing I was probably going to smother her, flung myself to the side, landing on the bed next to Mia with a thud.

"What. The. Fuck. Was that?" I gasped.

Mia turned her head to meet my gaze, her expression satisfied.

"Was it good for you?"

I smacked her shoulder lightly. "I thought you were supposed to be bad in bed? Holy crap. Did you ever do that to that chick from the restaurant?"

"Never."

"Her loss."

"It sure was."

The sex had been freaking incredible. We didn't have that awkward fumbling or any weird timing issues or nervousness that sometimes came with a new lover. Being friends first helped, because we were starting from a place of knowing each other's body language. But that wasn't all of it. The strength of our emotions added another layer that I hadn't experienced before with any other woman.

I fell asleep in Mia's arms, fully content in a way I hadn't been for a long time – if ever.

When I opened my eyes again, the sun was peeking through the curtains, bathing the room in light, and Mia was pressed against my back, one hand between my legs.

Sensing me waking up, she slid one of her legs between mine, separating my thighs so she could slip her questing fingers between my slippery folds. I ground against her hand and she rubbed her pelvis against my ass, taking her own pleasure as she got me off.

I reached behind me, moving my hand between us, searching until I found the engorged nub at her apex. Mia's hand in my pussy sped up, like she was frantic to get me to the finish line before she did, and I responded in kind. The sound of our slippery motions and rapid breathing filled the room, turning me on even more.

It only took a few minutes before my orgasm hit, this one more shallow and localized than the crashing full-body orgasm I'd experienced last night, but it was no less satisfying.

I cried out Mia's name as I found completion, grinding my pussy against her hand as I pushed my ass back into her. I felt her stiffen behind me, her mouth coming to bite down on my shoulder as she found her own release. As I fell back asleep with Mia wrapped around me, I had the thought that I could happily wake up like next to her every day for the rest of my life.

Mia

It had been three months since that night Colleen and I first acknowledged our feelings for each other, and I'd never been happier. We'd already been spending two or three nights a week together as friends, but now we were together any time either of us wasn't working.

We were inseparable. We went to yoga together. Hiked together. Watched movies together. And almost every day we brought each other pleasure. I was insatiable around Colleen, and she was the same around me. I'd never felt so desperate to have someone touch me, never been so focused on giving another person pleasure, never had so many orgasms in my damn life. It was an incredible experience.

Every Sunday we'd go together to attend Mass with my Mom, then have brunch with her. Mom and Colleen got along great, well enough that I'd started joking that Mom liked Colleen better than me. As I watched her soak up the maternal affection from my mother like a flower looking for water, it made me even sadder that Colleen had grown up in such a bad circumstances. The more she opened up about her parents, the more horrible they sounded.

I guess it was inevitable that our relationship would hit a rocky patch. Things had been going almost too well, and as my abuela would always say, "You need the salt to appreciate the sweet."

In this case, the salt came from a surprise run-in with Colleen's parents. Seattle was a major city, but it was small enough that sometimes it felt like a small town. One rainy and miserable Saturday, Colleen and I decided to go to the Frye Art Museum, since neither of us had been there before.

After walking around for several hours exploring the exhibits, we were ready to head out and get some food.

"I'm dying for a bacon cheeseburger!" Colleen said, just as we turned the corner for the lobby, walking hand in hand.

She came to a dead stop, her eyes fixed on an older couple coming from the other direction. It didn't take a rocket scientist to figure out they were her parents. She was a perfect mix of both of her parents, with her mother's slim and petite figure and her father's coloring and green eyes.

"Colleen Mary Murphy, is that you? I hardly recognized you with all that weight on you. And what's going on with your hair?"

Her mother's voice was shrill and judgmental, reminding me of how Colleen used to talk in high school. It made me slightly nauseous. For the record, Colleen was a size four, "all that weight" was a lie. I couldn't believe that after not seeing her daughter for fifteen years, this was how Mrs. Murphy greeted her.

Her father's gaze was fixed on our joined hands, disgust clear in his expression. Colleen started to pull away, but I tightened my fingers, subtly reminding her that we were a unit.

"Hi, I'm Mia, Colleen's girlfriend," I said when they all just stood there staring at each other.

Both of her parents ignored me, fixing their ire on their daughter.

"I'd hoped that by now Jesus would have helped you find your way past being an abomination," her father said, shaking his head like he was disappointed. "You're going to burn in hell, Colleen Mary, and that makes me sad."

"Look at her Patrick, she's clearly lost her way, gaining all that weight, being with women, and a Hispanic one at that." She said 'Hispanic' like it was a contagious disease. "Where did we go wrong?"

Colleen appeared to be in some dissociative state, so I gave her hand a firm tug, drawing her gaze to me.

"Where you went wrong was abusing your daughter," I said firmly. "The best thing she did was to get away from you disgusting bigoted assholes."

Colleen's parents stared at me in shock as I started to walk around them, bringing Colleen with me.

"Well, I would say it was nice running into you, but that would be a lie," I called over my shoulder. "Bye now."

Colleen didn't say a word the entire ride home from the museum. It was like she'd completely checked out. I'd never seen her like this before, and it scared the shit out of me.

I drove us back to her place. Normally we alternated between her apartment and mine, but I figured she'd feel more comfortable in a place that was familiar. I pulled up in front of her apartment and put the car in park, but Colleen didn't move.

"What do you need, babe? Do you want me to get some takeout?"

She pressed her hand against her stomach. "God no, I can't eat."

I felt a tiny bit of unease. The entire time I'd been friends with Colleen, she'd never once refused a meal.

"I just need to be alone. Please."

Now I was really worried.

"I don't know if that's a good idea, honey," I said softly. "Let me come in, even if you don't feel like talking. You seem really upset."

"Why would I be upset?"

She spun towards me, her face red and angry. It was better than that blank emotionless face she'd been wearing since we ran into her parents.

"Because I'm fat or because I'm going to burn in hell?"

"You don't believe any of that crap, do you?" I asked incredulously. "Your parents are horrible people. You can't let them get to you Colleen. You've worked hard for fifteen years to move past the way they treated you."

"I'm fine. I just need some time alone to think," she whispered, her arms folded protectively against her abdomen. I'd never seen her so lacking in confidence, looking so small and so dull.

"Okay, I'll call you later."

She didn't answer, she just got out of the car and raced towards the front door of her building. I watched her go, trying to decide what the best thing to do was, then deciding I should honor her wishes and leave her alone for a while. I wasn't happy about it, but she'd spent her whole childhood with people controlling her, ignoring her agency. I didn't want to be another person who did that to her, no matter how wrong it felt to drive away.

Colleen

My phone buzzed and I knew without looking that it was Mia. She'd called and texted me several times last night, but I hadn't answered. The only time I responded was when she messaged me early in the morning to ask if I was still coming to Mass with her and her mom.

I told her I was sick, and it wasn't a lie. My stomach was acidic like it was dissolving itself, and the fact that I hadn't eaten a bite of food in twenty-four hours wasn't helping. I knew logically that I needed to eat, that I'd worked so hard to learn how to nourish my body and not starve myself. But seeing my parents had just sent me right back to being fourteen and terrified that I'd end up fat and alone.

I needed to talk to my therapist, but it was Sunday so I wouldn't be able to reach her until tomorrow. Instead I lay on the couch, staring at the ceiling, my logical mind that had been honed through years of therapy fighting with the lizard part of my brain that was blaring, "Warning! Danger!"

Mid-afternoon I heard a knock on the door. I sighed and walked to the entryway.

"Go away Mia. Please, I'm not feeling up to talking," I called through the wood.

"Colleen, it's Juanita. Let me in please."

I reared back in shock. Mia had sent her Mom? I opened the door.

"Did Mia send you?"

Juanita laughed. "Goodness no, you know how she hates it when I interfere with her life. I'm here for you. Now move aside, I brought food."

My eyes snagged on the insulated bag in her hand. Mia's mom walked into the apartment, looking around.

"This place is very nice, I like it. Now come into the kitchen with me."

I guess I should have been offended by her bossy tone, but for some reason it was comforting. Juanita was a force of nature, the mother figure I'd never had.

"Sit down." She pointed at the kitchen table. "When was the last time you ate? No lying."

"Breakfast yesterday."

She made a tsking sound but only said, "We'll start with broth then."

I watched as she puttered around the kitchen, pouring some soup into a saucepan and heating it up. She placed a steaming mug of broth in front of me, then handed me a spoon.

"Have some bone broth, *mija*, it will restore your blood."

I took a spoonful, convinced I wasn't going to be able to eat it, but it tasted so delicious I eagerly took another. My entire body warmed from the inside. Juanita handed me a glass of water with watermelon chunks and mint leaves floating in the liquid. I'd had this drink before at her house, and always loved it.

"That's a good girl," Juanita said as I finished the soup. "We'll let that settle in your stomach while you tell me what's going on inside that pretty little head of yours."

Juanita must be the best social worker in Seattle, I thought, because suddenly I wanted to unload all my problems onto her. And I did, while she listened quietly. When I was done, she got up and took a pan out of the oven, bringing me a plate of chicken, vegetables, and Mexican rice.

"Now you eat while I talk."

I picked up my fork without an argument. The bone broth soup had both settled my stomach and whetted my appetite, and suddenly I was hungry.

"I never met your parents," Juanita started, "But I've known ever since you were a little girl that they are both very sick individuals."

My head popped up to stare at her.

"You won't remember this, but one time I got called to school when you and Mia were about eleven. The two of you had gotten into an argument about something, and it had turned into a fist fight. I came to pick up Mia and I saw you sitting in the lobby outside the principal's office, looking so thin and sad. You stretched, and your shirt rode up. I could see the marks on your back, like someone had hit you with a belt."

My fork clattered to the plate.

"I told the principal, and of course he blew me off. A man like that wasn't going to listen to a brown lady making allegations against some rich white people."

Juanita sighed deeply.

"As a social worker, I'm also a mandatory reporter, so I filed a child abuse complaint with the state. Unfortunately, like so many of these cases, your Mama and Daddy were able to charm the investigator, and when there were no more allegations raised by anyone after a year, they closed the case."

I closed my eyes, wondering what would have happened if someone – anyone – had taken Juanita's complaint seriously.

"You're eating, remember?" She nodded at my plate, and I dutifully resumed eating. As always, Juanita's food was delicious.

"I'm going to give you some tough love now Colleen. A lot of people have shitty parents. You're not that special in that regard. What makes you special is that you moved past it to create a life for yourself. Your parents took away your childhood, don't let them take away your adulthood."

She met my gaze. "Now quit wallowing. Enough is enough. Those awful people do not deserve any more space in your head."

My lips quirked. "You're right. Thank you, Juanita."

She stood up and moved around to give me a side hug. I closed my eyes, relaxing into her embrace.

"I'm glad you're with my daughter, but even if things don't work out between you two, you'll always have me."

"I love you."

"I love you too, *mija*. Like another daughter."

I turned to face her. "I'm in love with Mia."

Juanita patted my cheek. "I know you are, but I'm glad you figured that out on your own. Now be a good girl and finish your food."

Mia

Sunday night there was a knock on my door just after seven. I looked through the security peephole, surprised to find Colleen standing there. I hadn't seen her or talked to her in over twenty-four hours, and it was the longest we'd ever gone without contact since we'd started dating. I opened the door, letting her into my apartment.

"Hey."

She looked nervous, and I felt my stomach lurch. I'd unloaded the whole story on my Mom at brunch today, and she'd repeatedly assured me that it would work out for the best, but now I wasn't so sure.

"Are you here to break up with me?" I asked.

Colleen looked surprised.

"What? No. I'm here to tell you I love you."

"Huh?"

Colleen stepped closer, placing her hands on my shoulders. "I love you Mia. I'm sorry I blew you off yesterday, but I needed some time to think."

"And now you're done thinking?" I asked, still confused.

"Yep. Are you mad at me?"

"No. I'm just glad you're okay. Have you eaten something today?"

She smiled. "Yeah, your mom made me lunch."

"She did?"

"Yeah, she came over this afternoon and we talked for a while. It was helpful," she explained. "Then I told her I loved you and she said I should tell you that myself. But I needed to do a few things before I came over."

"Mom's a great person to talk things through with," I agreed. "Wait. Are you saying you told my Mom you loved me before you even told me?"

"Sorry, it just slipped out."

I nodded, and Colleen stared at me expectantly. "Um, do you have any response to that? Me saying I love you, I mean. No pressure if you don't, but I was just curious."

"Oh. Oh God, yeah. Sorry. I've said it so many times in my head I forgot that I never said it out loud."

"You still haven't said it out loud," she teased.

I stared into her eyes. "I love you, Colleen. I've loved you for a long time."

"Well don't take so long to tell me next time, I've been waiting and waiting for you to say it first."

"Well, I've been waiting for *you* to say it first," I countered.

"Aren't we just a pair of weirdos? Okay now that we've got that out of the way, how about make-up sex? I've got something I've been wanting to try."

Still feeling a little stunned, I followed Colleen into my bedroom. I realized that she had a backpack with her.

"What's all that?"

"I ordered some new toys." She pointed at the bed. "Get naked."

She didn't have to ask me twice. While we sometimes switched back and forth, Colleen generally liked to be in control in the bedroom. I didn't mind that. She'd never disappointed me yet.

Reaching into her bag, Colleen pulled out some kind of large appliance with a long cord.

"What the hell is that?"

She moved to the bedside table, pulling it out from the wall so she could reach the outlet.

"It's the original Magic Wand, the most powerful of the vibrators."

I looked at the bulbous head on what looked like a back massager.

"There's no way that's getting up in here," I said, pointing at my now-naked pussy. The Magic Wand was enormous.

"Trust me."

I lay on the bed, and Colleen pulled out two long scarves. Without a word, she secured one to each of my wrists and then tied my hands to the headboard slats.

"We've never done bondage before," I reminded her.

"Yeah, but I've always wanted to, so today seemed like a good day to try it."

"Will you be taking off your clothes at any time?" I asked, nodding at her yoga pants, tank top, and hoodie.

"In a bit."

She turned on the vibrator and we both startled. That damn thing was super loud. But then I forgot all about the sound because she started sliding the Magic Wand up and down the outside of my pussy, the powerful vibrations drawing all my attention.

Slowly, she slipped it in between my pussy lips. "Damn, that thing is strong."

She just smiled as she started moving up and down my slit with the head of the vibrating wand. I went from zero to about to lose my shit in about thirty seconds. It was ten times more powerful than any vibe I'd tried, and I'd seriously never gotten so aroused so quickly. My hips bucked, trying to escape the vibrations as I pulled uselessly at my bound wrists.

Colleen shifted so she was sitting between my legs, her legs spread wide to pin down my own legs. Returning the focus of the vibrator to my clit, I whined, realizing I had nowhere to go to escape.

"It's too much," I whimpered.

"You can take it," she said confidently.

She circled my clit over and over again, alternating between large light circles and more direct pressure at the center. The vibrations reverberated through my entire pelvis, until I came with a long piercing scream. I shook violently, unable to move with my body pinned down. To my shock, I came so hard that I actually squirted.

"That was awesome!" Colleen laughed delightedly, moving the vibe away and turning it off.

I sagged against the bed, feeling completely boneless. I stared at the ceiling, shellshocked and overwhelmed by the sensations moving through my body. It still felt like my pelvis was vibrating, and I was having little orgasm aftershocks deep in my core.

"Holy. Fuck." I finally gasped.

Colleen crawled over me to release my hands from the scarves and as soon as I was free, I pulled her down on top of me, giving her an ardent kiss. When she lifted her head, I cupped her cheeks in my hands and stared into her green eyes.

"Once I have control of my limbs, we're going to try that again, but with you this time," I said. "That toy definitely needs to go into the rotation."

Colleen shifted to my side, cuddling against me. "That sounds like a good plan."

"You know what else sounds like a good plan?" I asked.

"What?"

"Forever."

"Oh good. Because forever sounds good to me too."

Epilogue – Colleen

Valentine's Day, one year later...

"I can't believe you want me to come back to the restaurant where I was humiliated last Valentine's Day," Mia grumbled as we walked up the street.

I squeezed her hand. "It's also the restaurant where we met again and started to fall in love," I reminded her. "It's special to us."

"If you say so," I teased.

Neither Mia nor I were gushy romantics, but at some point we'd decided that Valentine's Day was our anniversary—even though we technically hadn't started dating until a few months after we reconnected.

Arriving at the restaurant, we hung up our coats on the rack, and I took a moment to look at the woman I loved. She was wearing a red velvet dress, in a nod to both the holiday and the below freezing temperatures Seattle was experiencing. The dress hugged her curves and fell to just below her knee, where the hem skimmed the top of her knee-high boots.

I'd gone with a jade green dress that brought out the green in my eyes. I'd put on about five pounds over the last year, and to my delight, it all seemed to settle in my chest and hips, giving me a little more of a curvy shape. Twenty years ago, gaining five pounds would send me into a shame spiral of exercise and food deprivation, but now I could recognize that a little bit more weight looked good on me. It made me look more womanly. And Mia certainly seemed to appreciate the extra meat on my bones, given that she couldn't keep her hands off me despite almost nine months of officially dating.

Just like last year, the restaurant was packed with couples here to enjoy a date night for the holiday.

We ordered the special Valentine's Day cocktails, pomegranate martinis. After some discussion, did what we often did when we ate out

"

together: we each ordered an entrée that we then shared with the other so we could each enjoy half of two different entrees and not have to choose just one. Tonight we shared a steak and an order of lobster, which seemed fitting for our anniversary celebration. The past year had been something to celebrate for sure.

"How about dessert?" I asked.

"I'm stuffed," Mia said.

I felt a surge of alarm. We needed to order dessert.

"We should share a chocolate mousse," I suggested. "That's nice and light."

"Okay, that would be good." Mia gave me a weird look. It wasn't like me to push food on someone.

I made eye contact with our waiter, and he hurried over. I'd planned this out carefully, and he was in on the plan. It was another reason that I'd chosen this restaurant for our Valentine's Day date: they knew me here since I was a regular.

"Yes ma'am?"

"We'd like to share a chocolate mousse please."

The waiter gave me a smile.

"Good choice. The mousse is particularly good this evening."

He returned a few minutes later with a tall glass dish filled with chocolate mousse and topped with whipped cream. I slid it over to Mia.

"You can have the whipped cream."

Mia loved whipped cream. Sometimes when she had a particularly bad day working with the kids at the hospital, she would come home and squirt it from the can directly into her mouth.

She scooped up the small dollop of whipped cream and brought the spoon to her mouth.

"What the hell?" She stared at the whipped cream on her spoon. "There's something in here."

That was my cue. I stood up and dropped to one knee next to the table. Everyone around us turned to watch.

"What are you...oh. Oh!"

Mia fished the engagement ring out of the whipped cream, wiping it with her napkin to reveal the silver band with a small emerald. Juanita had helped me pick it out, and we'd both agreed that Mia would not like some big flashy diamond.

I grabbed her hand.

"Mia Hernandez, love of my life, would you marry me?"

Mia looked from the ring in her hand to my face for a long, nerve wracking moment before her face broke out in the biggest smile I'd ever seen.

"Yes! Yes, I will marry you Colleen Murphy."

We both leapt to our feet, meeting in the middle for a kiss that had our fellow patrons clapping for us. As we pulled apart, I slid the ring on her left hand, and we both admired it.

"This emerald is almost the same color as your eyes," she said, a tone of wonder in her voice.

"How about we get out of here and get a drink?" I asked, repeating the words I'd uttered last year. The words that had changed the course of both of our lives.

"How about we get out of here and go have engaged people sex?" she countered.

"I like the way you think."

***

Check out the story of how Miranda and Elizabeth got together in "My College Crush", available everywhere[1] now.

If you liked this book, please consider leaving a review or rating to let me know. You can find more of Reba's lesbian romances on her website at bit.ly/AuthorRebaBale[2].

---

1. https://books2read.com/u/bOy8aJ

2. *https://books2read.com/ap/nB2qJv/Reba-Bale*

Be sure to join my newsletter for more great books. You'll receive a copy of my book "Hotwife Happy Hour" for free when you join my newsletter. Subscribers are the first to hear about all of my new releases and sales. Visit my mailing list sign-up[3] at bit.ly/rebabooks to get your free book today.

---

3.   https://storyoriginapp.com/giveaways/495308f4-2d9f-11ed-bfd5-c7ccde0cb7e8

Special Preview

The Divorcee's First Time
A Contemporary Lesbian Romance
By Reba Bale

"It's done," I said triumphantly. "My divorce is final."

My best friend Susan paused in the process of sliding into the restaurant booth, her sharply manicured eyebrows raising almost to her hairline. "Dickhead finally signed the papers?" she asked, her tone hopeful.

I nodded as Susan settled into the seat across from me. "The judge signed off on it today. Apparently his barely legal girlfriend is knocked up, and she wants to get a ring on her finger before the big event." I explained with a touch of irony in my voice. "The child bride finally got it done for me."

Susan smiled and nodded. "Well congratulations and good riddance. Let's order some wine."

We were most of the way through our second bottle when the conversation turned back to my ex. "I wonder if Dickhead and his Child Bride will last for the long haul," Susan mused.

I shook my head and blew a chunk of hair away from my mouth.

"I doubt it," I told her. "Someday she's gonna roll over and think, there's got to be something better out there than a self-absorbed man child who doesn't know a clitoris from a doorknob."

Susan laughed, sputtering her wine. I eyed her across the table. Although she was ten years older than me, we had been best friends for the last five years. We worked together at the accounting firm. She had been my trainer when I first came there, fresh out of school with my degree. We bonded over work, but soon realized that we were kindred spirits.

Susan was rapidly approaching 40 but could easily pass for my age. Her hair was black and shiny, hinting at her Puerto Rican heritage, with blunt bangs and blond highlights that she paid a fortune for. Her face was clear and unlined, with large brown eyes and cheek bones that could cut glass. She was an avid runner and worked hard to maintain a slim physique since the women in her family ran towards the chunkier side.

I was almost her complete opposite. Blonde curls to her straight dark hair, blue eyes instead of brown, curvy where she was lean, introverted to her extrovert.

But somehow, we clicked. We were closer than sisters. Honestly, I don't know how I would have gotten through the last year without her. She had been the first one I called when my marriage fell apart, and she had supported me throughout the whole process.

It had been a big shock when I came home early one day and found my husband getting a blow job in the middle of our living room. It had been even more shocking when I saw the fresh young face at the other end of that blow job.

"What the fuck are you doing?" I had screeched, startling them both out of their sex stupor. "You're getting blow jobs from children now?"

The girl had looked up from her knees with eyes glowing in righteous indignation. "I'm not a child, I'm nineteen," she had informed me proudly. "I'm glad you finally found out. I give him what you don't, and he loves me."

I looked into the familiar eyes of my husband and saw the panic and confusion there. I made it easy for him. "Get out," I told him firmly, my voice leaving no room for argument. "Take your teenage girlfriend and get the fuck out. We're getting a divorce. Expect to hear from my lawyer."

The condo was in my name. I had purchased it before we were married, and since I had never added his name to the deed, he had no rights to it. There was no question he would be the one leaving.

My husband just stared at me with his jaw hanging open like he couldn't believe it. "But Jennifer," he whined. "You don't understand. Let me explain."

"There's nothing to understand," I told him sadly. "This is a deal breaker for me, and you know that as well as I do. We are done."

The girl had taken his hand and smiled triumphantly. "Come on baby," she told him. "Zip up and let's get out of here. We can finally be together like we planned."

"Yeah baby," I had sneered. "I'll box up your stuff. It'll be in the hallway tomorrow. Pick it up by six o'clock or I'm trashing it all."

After they left my first call was to the locksmith, but my second call was to Susan.

That night was the last time I had seen my husband until we had met for the court-ordered pre-divorce mediation. He spent most of that session reiterating what he had told me in numerous voice mails, emails and sessions spent yelling on the other side of my front door. He loved me. He had made a terrible mistake. He wasn't going to sign the papers. We were meant to be together. Needless to say, mediation hadn't been very successful. Fortunately, I had been careful to keep our assets separate, as if I knew that someday I would be in this situation.

Through it all, Susan had been my rock. In the end I don't think I was even that sad about the divorce, I was really angrier with myself for staying in a relationship that wasn't fulfilling with a man I didn't love anymore.

"You need to get some quality sex." Susan drew my attention back to the present. "Bang him out of your system."

"I don't know," I answered slowly. "I think I need a hiatus."

"A hiatus from what?" Susan asked with a frown. "You haven't had sex in what, eighteen months?"

I nodded. "Yeah, but I just can't take a disappointing fumble right now. I would rather have nothing than another three-pump chump."

I shook my head and continued, "I'm going to stick with my battery-operated boyfriend, he never disappoints me."

Susan smiled. "That's because you know your way around your own vajayjay."

She motioned to the waiter to bring us a third bottle of wine.

"That's why I like to date women," she continued. "We already know our way around the equipment."

I nodded thoughtfully. "You make a good point."

Susan leaned forward. "We've never talked about this," she said earnestly. "Have you ever been with a woman?"

For more of the story, check out "The Divorcee's First Time" by Reba Bale, available for immediate [1]<u>purchase</u> today.

***

Want a free book? Join my newsletter and receive a free copy of my book "Hotwife Happy Hour" for free. I'll contact you a few times a month with story updates, new releases, and special sales. Go to bit.ly/rebabooks to sign up today.

Other Books by Reba Bale

Check out my other books, available on most major online retailers now. Go to my webpage[1] to learn more.

Friends to Lovers Lesbian Romance Series

The Divorcee's First Time
My BFF's Sister
My Rockstar Assistant
My College Crush
My Fake Girlfriend
My Secret Crush
My Holiday Love
My Valentine's Gift
My Spring Fling

Menage Romances

Pie Promises
Tornado Warning
Summer in Paradise
Life of the Mardi

Hotwife Erotic Romances

Hotwife in the Woods
Hotwife on the Beach
Hotwife Under the Tree
A Hotwife's Retreat

The Marriage Survival Series

Finding His Alpha: A Wife's First Spanking
Watching His Wife: The First Time Sharing
Exploring His Fantasy: A First Time Gay Ménage

---

1. https://books2read.com/ap/nB2qJv/Reba-Bale

The Divorce Recovery Series

The Spanking Therapy Series

Unlikely Doms Series

The Voyeur Romance Series

Paying for Tuition

Toys for Grown-Ups Series

Punishing Holidays

Other Standalone Stories

Sinful Desires

The Ride of My Life

Taken by Surprise

Share Me: A Cheating Husband's Punishment

Want a free book? Join my newsletter and receive a free copy of my book "Hotwife Happy Hour" for free. You'll be the first to hear about new releases or special sales, so visit bit.ly/rebabooks to sign up today.

About the Author

Reba Bale loves writing naughty stories where the characters are able to tap into their inner fantasies and experience spanking, bondage, humiliation, or other activities on the non-vanilla side of life. When Reba is not writing she is reading the same naughty stories she likes to write.

You can also follow Reba on Medium[2] for free stories, bonus epilogues and more. You can also hear all about new releases and special sales by joining Reba's newsletter mailing list.[3]

---

2.   https://medium.com/@authorrebabale

3.   https://bit.ly/rebabooks

Don't miss out!

Visit the website below and you can sign up to receive emails whenever Reba Bale publishes a new book. There's no charge and no obligation.

https://books2read.com/r/B-A-IDTM-YWJFC

BOOKS 2 READ

Connecting independent readers to independent writers.

Did you love *My Valentine's Gift*? Then you should read *My College Crush*[4] by Reba Bale!

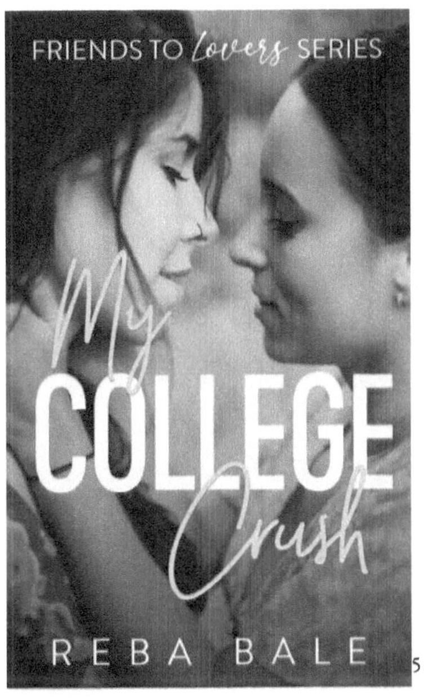

She kissed a girl...and then the girl married a man. Miranda and Elizabeth were best friends throughout college. They shared everything: the same dorm room, the same group of friends, the same major. Until the night that their friendship became something more, and they shared their first lesbian experience. The next morning Elizabeth was gone, leaving only a note. She transferred schools and married the "perfect" man her rich parents picked out for her. Other than glimpses in the society pages, Miranda never heard from her again.Fifteen years later Miranda walks into a Lesbian Spirituality Retreat in the mountains and to her complete shock, one of the other participants is Elizabeth, the woman who broke her heart all those years ago.Elizabeth spent ten years

---

4. https://books2read.com/u/bOy8aJ

5. https://books2read.com/u/bOy8aJ

of her life married to a man she didn't love and keeping up appearances for her controlling parents. When she finally broke away, they disowned her. But now she's living life on her own terms: reading tarot cards, doing yoga, eating vegetarian, and dating women. Seeing Miranda again is like finding the missing piece of her soul. But after the way she broke her friend's heart, she's going to have to work hard to convince the other woman that she's changed and ready to commit to a long-term love with her college crush."My College Crush" is book four in the "Friends to Lovers" romantic novella series. Each book in the series is a steamy standalone featuring an LGBTQ couple making the leap from friends to lovers and looking for their "happily ever after".

Also by Reba Bale

Affair Recovery
Share Me: A Cheating Husband's Punishment

Dancing with Strangers
Taken by Surprise

Friends to Lovers
The Divorcee's First Time: A Hot Friends-to-Lovers Lesbian Romance
My BFF's Sister
My Rockstar Assistant
My College Crush
My Fake Girlfriend
My Secret Crush
My Holiday Love
My Valentine's Gift
My Spring Fling

Paying for Tuition

The Billionaire's Assistant
The Babysitter's Ride Home
The Babysitter's First Ménage
The Teaching Assistant's Lesson

Punishing Holidays
Turkey and a Spanking
Shopping and a Spanking

Sharing With Strangers
The Ride of My Life

Spanking Therapy Clinic
The Reluctant Bride's First Spanking
The Reluctant Bride Gets Caught
The Billionaire Gets Punished
The Curvy Reporter Gets Punished

The Divorce Recovery Team
Spanking Justice
A Punishing Workout
A Disciplined Budget

The Marriage Survival Retreat
Finding His Alpha

Watching His Wife
Exploring His Fantasy

The Voyeur Romance Series
Naughty Dinner Date
Naughty Laundry Day
Naughty Camping
Naughty Love Story
Naughty Sunbathing

Toys for Grown-Ups
Ménage a Geek
Financial Punishment

Unlikely Doms
Alpha in a Sweater Vest
Alpha Student
Alpha Yogi

Standalone
Hotel Spanking
Unlikely Doms
Divorce Recovery Team: A Punishment Experiment Collection
Spicing Up My Marriage
It Takes Three
The Christmas Swap

Sinful Desires